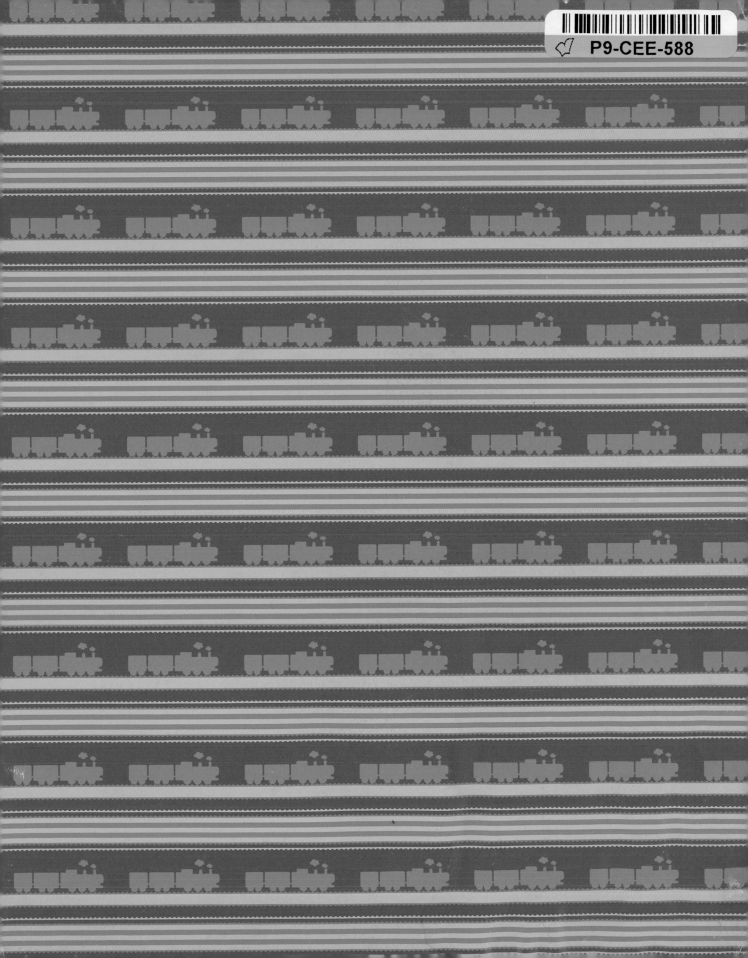

10 11 12 13 14 15 16 17 18 19 20

Library of Congress Cataloging-in-Publication Data
Awdry, W.
Thomas and the shooting star / based on The railway series by the Rev. W. Awdry ;
illustrated by Tommy Stubbs.
p.   cm.
"Thomas the tank engine & friends. A Britt Allcroft Company production."
SUMMARY: Unable to fall asleep, Thomas the tank engine
goes on a nighttime adventure in search of a shooting star.
ISBN 0-375-81523-6
[1. Meteors—Fiction. 2. Stars—Fiction.
3. Railroads—Trains—Fiction. 4. Bedtime—Fiction.]
I. Stubbs, Tommy, ill. II. Thomas the tank engine and friends.
III. Title. PZ7 .A9613 Tg 2002 [E]—dc21   2001041876

www.randomhouse.com/kids
www.thomasthetankengine.com

Printed in Italy First Edition April 2002 10 9

THOMAS & FRIENDS™

Thomas and the Shooting Star

Illustrated by Tommy Stubbs

Random House 🏠 New York

Thomas the Tank Engine & Friends

A BRITT ALLCROFT COMPANY PRODUCTION
Based on The Railway Series by the Rev W Awdry
© Gullane (Thomas) LLC 2002
Published in the United States by Random House, Inc., New York, and simultaneously in
Canada by Random House of Canada Limited, Toronto.

It was way past Thomas' bedtime and the other engines were all sleeping in the shed. Thomas couldn't fall asleep.

"Pssst! Gordon, are you asleep?" Thomas peeped.

The big blue engine opened one eye. "Thomas, it's the middle of the night. Big engines like me need their sleep, and so do you."

"I can't sleep," said Thomas, "and I've tried everything. . . . I counted sheep. . . . I whistled my favorite song over and over. . . . I had some warm oil. And I'm still not sleepy."

At that very moment, a bright light blazed a path across the sky. It was the prettiest thing Thomas had ever seen.

"What was *that*?" Thomas asked Gordon.

"A shooting star," replied Gordon sleepily. Then Gordon decided to play a joke on Thomas. "A shooting star," he said, "is a star that runs through the sky telling the other stars how to get to sleep. You should try to catch up with it, Thomas . . . maybe it will tell you how to fall asleep!"

"Wow! Thanks, Gordon, I think I will," said
Thomas. Then quietly, so as not to wake the other
engines, he crept out of the shed and set out after the
shooting star.

"Now *I* can get some sleep." Gordon smiled sleepily
and closed his eyes.

Thomas steamed down the tracks and through the countryside. To get a better view, he puffed to the top of a nearby hill. There were lots of twinkling stars in the sky, but not the shooting star.

When he looked down the track, he saw a bright light in the distance moving toward him.

"There it is!" he peeped happily. "It's coming to tell me how to get to sleep!"

Thomas chugged toward the light, but it wasn't the shooting star after all. It was Percy, pulling the night mail train.

"Hello, Percy," Thomas sighed.

"Thomas, what are *you* doing out at this time of night?" Percy asked. "Isn't it past your bedtime?"

"I couldn't sleep," Thomas replied, "and then I saw a shooting star. It was so pretty. Did you see it?"

"I've been busy delivering the mail," Percy answered. "The only thing *I've* seen is all these bags of letters and parcels I have to deliver!"

"Well, I am going to catch up to the shooting star, and it is going to tell me how to get to sleep! Gordon told me so!" And Thomas hurried past Percy and down the track.

"Oh, no, Thomas . . . ," Percy called.

But Thomas didn't hear him.

"It has to be somewhere," Thomas insisted as he chugged past fields and farms.

Suddenly something landed on his roof! Could it be the shooting star? Thomas slowed to a crawl and looked up.

A large owl was on his roof.

"Hello, owl," Thomas said. "Did you see a shooting star go by?"

"Noohooo! Noohooo!" said the owl.

"Bust my boiler!" puffed Thomas, startling the owl. "Well, I'm going to find it, and it will tell me how to get to sleep," Thomas went on as the owl flew off.

"A shooting star can't just disappear, can it?" he thought as he looked up in the sky.

Just then, down the tracks and over the hills, Thomas saw a light moving across the sky.

"There it is!" he cried, and he raced ahead.

But it wasn't the shooting star. It was Thomas' friend Harold.

"Thomas, what are *you* doing out at this time of night? Isn't it past your bedtime?" Harold asked.

"I couldn't sleep, and then I saw a shooting star," Thomas replied. "Gordon said I should find it and ask it how to get to sleep. Did you see it go by?"

Harold chuckled. "Gordon was teasing you, Thomas," he said kindly. "Shooting stars are too far away and too fast for any engine to catch, even a Really Useful Engine like yourself. Why don't you go back to the shed and go to sleep? It's *very* late. I'm just going back to the airfield to get some rest myself."

"But I'm *not* tired," Thomas grumped as Harold flew off. "Drat that Gordon!"

Then he gave a big yawn. "Well, maybe I am a *little* tired."

Thomas slowly started back to the shed. The whole way home, he tried to think of some trick to pay Gordon back, but he was so tired he could barely keep his eyes on the track.

Finally, he rolled into the yard.

Edward was awake. "Where have you been?" he asked.

"Oh, Edward, I couldn't sleep and I saw a shooting star," said Thomas. "Gordon told me if I caught the star, it would tell me how to fall asleep. Then I saw Harold, who told me that Gordon was tricking me." Thomas yawned again.

"Maybe you didn't catch the star, but you certainly look sleepy," said Edward.

"Hey, that's right." Thomas smiled as his eyes drooped shut. "Gordon was kind of right after all."

Edward laughed. "Well, if Gordon said that by chasing a shooting star you'd learn how to fall asleep, he certainly seems to have been right."

But Thomas didn't hear him. He was already sound asleep.

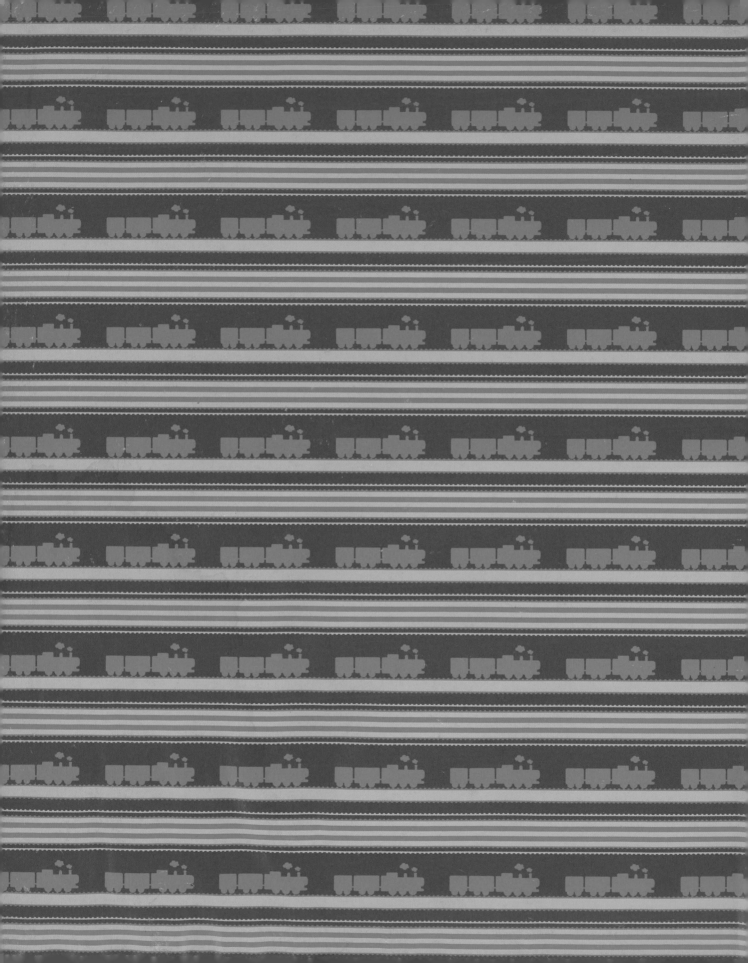